DEC 1 8 2017

Jake Drake

CLASS CLOWN

Jake Drake
CLASS CLOWN

Andrew Clements
illustrated by Dolores Avendaño

SIMON & SCHUSTER BOOKS FOR YOUNG READERS

New York   London   Toronto   Sydney   Singapore

For Priscilla Avery,
the best neighbor a first-year teacher ever had
—A. C.

SIMON & SCHUSTER BOOKS FOR YOUNG READERS
An imprint of Simon & Schuster Children's Publishing Division
1230 Avenue of the Americas, New York, New York 10020

SIMON & SCHUSTER BOOKS FOR YOUNG READERS is a trademark of
Simon & Schuster.

Book design by Lisa Vega
The text of this book was set in ITC Century Book.
The illustrations were rendered in pen and ink.

Printed in the United States of America

13

0710RR2

ISBN-13: 978-0-689-83921-4
ISBN-10: 0-689-83921-9

Library of Congress Control Number: 2001098274

Contents

NEW BOSS

I'm Jake, Jake Drake. I'm only ten years old, but I already have a full-time job. Because that's sort of how I think about school. It's my job.

I'm in fourth grade now, so I've had the same job for more than five years. And if you do something long enough, you get pretty good at it. That's how come I'm starting to be an expert about school.

I've had a bunch of different bosses so far. Because that's what a teacher is: the boss. And one thing I know for sure is that it's no fun when your boss is a sourpuss.

So far things have been okay for me. A few of my teachers have gotten grumpy now and then, and a couple of them have really yelled once in a while. And this year my fourth-grade teacher is Mr. Thompson, who can get grouchy sometimes. Plus he has brown hair growing out of his ears. So he might be a werewolf.

Still, I've never had a real sourpuss for a teacher—at least not for a whole school year.

But not Willie. Willie's my best friend, and last year his third-grade teacher was Mrs. Frule. She's one of those bosses who walks around with this mad look on her face, sort of like a cat when it's outside in the rain. If you go past her room, you feel like you should whisper and walk on tiptoe. Because if Mrs. Frule even looks at you, she can always find something to get mad about.

So third grade was tough for Willie because he's the kind of kid who loves to smile. Putting Mrs. Frule and Willie into the same classroom was a bad idea.

When I met Willie at lunch on our first day of third grade, I could tell something was wrong. He looked sort of pale, like maybe he was going to keel over or something. I said, "Hey, are you okay?"

And he said, "No, I'm *not* okay. Mrs. Frule already hates me. I spent half the morning getting yelled at, and the other half trying to figure out what I was doing wrong."

I asked, "What happened?"

Willie shrugged. "That's what I don't get. I didn't *do* anything. I was just sitting there, and all of a sudden I saw Mrs. Frule looking at me. So I smiled at her, and she frowned and said, 'Young man, wipe that smile off your face.' So I did. I wiped my hand across my mouth like this, and I stopped smiling. But that made Robbie Kenson start laughing, so then Mrs. Frule got real mad and she made me get up and walk out into the hall. And then she came out and leaned down, like, right into my face. She got so close I could see all the way up her nose. And she shook her finger at me and said, 'If you ever act like a smart aleck in my classroom again, you are going to be very, very sorry!'"

Poor guy. That was only Willie's first day of third grade, and it didn't get any better. All year long Mrs. Frule yelled at Willie at least three times a week. And he's one of the *good* kids! The kids like Jay Karnes and Zack Walton—real troublemakers? For those guys, being in Mrs. Frule's class was sort of like being in a prison camp. Maybe worse, because in a prison camp, if you mess up, you don't have to get a note signed by your parents.

My third-grade teacher was Mrs. Snavin, and she was pretty nice most of the time. I wished Willie could have switched to my class. But it doesn't work that way. Once school starts, you're stuck with your teacher for the whole year, and you just have to make the best of it.

And that's what Willie did. He didn't have a lot of fun in third grade, but he lived through it. Even Jay and Zack survived. Because that's what you do when your teacher is a grumphead. You learn what you have to do to stay alive, and you do it. And you know that once the year is over, you'll never have that boss again. So you just do your best and wait for summer.

Like I said, most of my teachers have been pretty nice. Actually, the grumpiest teacher I've had so far wasn't even a teacher. She was a student teacher. And I didn't have her for that long. Only about three weeks. Which was plenty. Her name was Miss Bruce.

Miss Bruce showed up on a Monday morning in April near the end of second grade. Mrs. Brattle was my regular teacher that year, and she said, "This is Miss Bruce. She's in college, and she's studying to be a teacher. As part of her college work, she's going to be here in our classroom for a while."

I looked at Miss Bruce. She was younger than Mrs. Brattle. A lot younger. She was so young that she sort of looked like Link Baxter's big sister. Except Link's sister was only in high school. Plus part of her hair was colored pink. Or sometimes purple.

Miss Bruce's hair was reddish blond. That first day she had on a blue shirt and a green skirt and blue shoes. Her nose was kind of small. Or maybe her nose was mostly hidden, because she wore a big pair of glasses with black rims. And her nose had freckles, too.

For her first three days Miss Bruce didn't do

much. Sometimes she helped Mrs. Brattle pass out papers. Once she read part of a story out loud. But most of the time she just sat in a chair near the back of the room and watched.

By Wednesday we'd gotten used to her hanging around. No one paid much attention to Miss Bruce. Except me. I kept looking at her during those first three days.

And I noticed something.

Back in second grade, Willie and I were both in Mrs. Brattle's class, so at lunch on Wednesday I asked Willie a question. I asked, "Have you noticed anything funny about Miss Bruce?"

"Funny?" said Willie. "You mean like the way she squints and wrinkles her nose when she looks at the chalkboard? I think that's kind of funny, don't you?"

"No," I said, "I mean funny like strange. Have you ever seen her smile?"

Willie was scraping the icing off an Oreo with his front teeth. He stopped right in the middle of the cookie. His eyes opened wide and he said, "You're right! I haven't seen her smile at all! Have you?"

I shook my head. "Nope. Not once. I wonder why."

Willie finished his first scrape and then started licking the leftovers. He stopped with his tongue sticking out. Then he gulped real fast and said, "Hey! Maybe she *can't* smile! Maybe she has a special problem, like if she smiles, her teeth fall out or something! Or maybe . . . maybe she's . . . an *alien!* Yeah, she's an alien, and she doesn't know how to smile, and . . . and she's going to use her special powers . . . to turn all of us into hamburgers and beam us up to her spaceship!"

Willie's like that. He has a lot of imagination.

But in a way, Willie was right. Miss Bruce *did* seem to have some special powers.

And there was one power she had that was going to change my life for a while. Because Miss Bruce was about to turn me into Jake Drake, Class Clown.

CHAPTER TWO

SCARED STIFF

Thursday morning Mrs. Brattle asked us all to be quiet and listen. She asked Miss Bruce to come and stand next to her at the front of the classroom. Then Mrs. Brattle said, "For the next several weeks, Miss Bruce is going to be your teacher. I'm going to be helping Mrs. Reed in the library during this time, so I'll probably see you every day. And I'll even be here in the classroom sometimes. But Miss Bruce will be your teacher. I want all of you to be on your very best behavior for her."

And then Mrs. Brattle picked up her purse and a stack of papers and walked out of the room.

We all sat at our tables and looked at Miss Bruce. And Miss Bruce stood there at the front of the room and looked at us. Then she said, "Let's begin by talking about the rules." Her voice sounded kind of high and squeaky. "First of all, it is going to be quiet in my classroom. No talking, no whispering, and no shouting or laughing. You may not talk unless you raise your hand first and I give you permission. We have a lot of work to do, and we don't have time for any fooling around. I have very high expectations for each one of you, and I'm going to demand excellence. Is that clear?"

Miss Bruce lifted up her eyebrows, all the way above her big glasses. And she looked around the class. And she didn't smile.

I looked around too and I could see this look on everyone's face. Sort of a scared look. Even Link Baxter looked scared, and that almost never happened.

Then Miss Bruce clapped her hands together twice and said, "All right. Now. Let's not waste

any time. Please get out your math workbooks."

Laura Pell raised her hand. When Miss Bruce nodded at her, Laura said, "We always have reading before math."

Miss Bruce didn't smile. She said, "What's your name?"

"Laura."

Miss Bruce said, "Laura, I want you to answer a question for me, all right?"

In a real small voice Laura said, "Okay."

"Now, Laura," said Miss Bruce, "who is your teacher?"

Laura smiled, because that was an easy question. She said, "My teacher is Mrs. Brattle."

Miss Bruce raised her eyebrows and leaned forward, and she said, "Now, Laura, please think. What did Mrs. Brattle just say? Who is your teacher for the next few weeks?"

In a tiny little voice Laura said, "You are."

Miss Bruce nodded at her and said, "That's right, Laura, *I* am your teacher now. And what did I ask you to do a minute ago?"

Laura said, "You said to get out our math workbooks."

Miss Bruce nodded. "And now I'm going to say it again: Class, please get out your math workbooks."

So we did. We all got out our math workbooks. Then we turned to page 47 like Miss Bruce told us to, and we did some addition problems. There was no talking. There was no whispering. There was no looking out the window. And there was no smiling.

We took the worksheet out of the workbook when Miss Bruce told us to. We wrote our names on our papers when Miss Bruce told us to. Then we passed in the papers. Quietly.

Then it was time for social studies. We had to read three pages in our *People and Places* book. Quietly. And then answer some questions on page 83. We had to write down our answers with no talking and no looking at our neighbors' papers. That's what Miss Bruce said. Like she thought we might cheat. And she didn't smile.

I looked over at Laura Pell. Her face didn't move, sort of like she was wearing a mask. She sat up straight in her chair. She didn't smile at all. She kept her eyes looking down at her table.

When she was done with her work, she folded her hands and put them in her lap. She looked like a statue.

And I knew why Laura was acting that way. She was scared of making a mistake. She was scared of Miss Bruce—scared stiff. Because when you get a grumphead for a boss, that can happen. And if your boss is grumpy and fussy and picky all at once, it's extra scary.

It was so quiet in our classroom. All I could hear was the squeaking of Miss Bruce's blue shoes as she walked around the room.

I took a quick look at the rest of the kids. Willie was scared. And Andrea Selton. Everyone was scared stiff, even Ben Grumson, who was even tougher to scare than Link Baxter.

And so was I. I sat still. Willie was sitting at my table, just two feet away, but I never looked at him. Because I was afraid we might smile at each other and get caught. And then Miss Bruce might get mad at us.

A part of me had decided to be careful. Part of me wanted to make sure there wasn't any trouble.

But there was another part of me that didn't

want to sit there like a bag of potatoes. This other part of me didn't want to just fold my hands and look down at my desk.

There was a part of me that didn't care if Miss Bruce got mad. That was the part of me that wanted to stand on my head and stick out my tongue and yell, really loud.

But did I?

No. That first day when Miss Bruce took over our class, I didn't dare.

I was too scared, just like everyone else.

CHAPTER THREE

SCARED SILLY

I'm usually happy on Friday mornings.

Friday means that the next day is Saturday, and on most Saturdays Willie and I mess around together. We watch some TV. We ride our bikes, play some computer games, and mostly have fun. If the weather's good, we work on our fort in the woods behind Willie's house. So Friday means work is almost over for the week.

But the Friday after Miss Bruce took over, I didn't feel happy. It felt like it was going to be the hardest day of my life.

On the bus ride to school that day, I thought, *Maybe Miss Bruce will be nicer today. Maybe she'll smile a little. Today will probably be a lot better than yesterday.*

I was wrong.

Friday started off like Thursday had. First we did a math worksheet. Instead of passing them in, we exchanged papers. Miss Bruce read the right answers for us. And she never smiled.

Then we did a map-skills sheet for social studies. We marked North, South, East, and West. We colored the rivers and lakes blue. We found the railroads and the highways. We found the mountains and the cities. Then Miss Bruce turned on the overhead projector and showed us how our maps should look. She said we could fix our maps if we had any mess-ups. That was sort of nice of her, but she never smiled.

Gym was great. Not because I love gym, because most of the time I don't. Gym was great because Miss Bruce wasn't there.

After gym, we all went back to class. There was no laughing, and nobody was late, not even one second.

Then Miss Bruce said we were going to have a spelling bee, and everyone was glad. Spelling bees are always fun, right? Wrong. Not when Miss Bruce is the boss.

Miss Bruce looked down at the seating chart and then looked through her big glasses at Meaghan Wright. She said, "You'll be first, Meaghan. Remember the rules: You have to say the word, then spell it, and then say it again. Ready?"

Meaghan nodded, so Miss Bruce said, "The first word is 'mouse.'"

Meaghan looked up at the ceiling. Then she took a deep breath and said, "M-o- . . ."

Miss Bruce shook her head and said, "Please stop."

Real fast, Meaghan said, "Oh, oh—I know. I forgot to say the word first, right? Mouse; m-o- . . ."

Shaking her head, Miss Bruce said, "I'm sorry, Meaghan, but you didn't follow the rules, and it's important that we all learn to follow directions exactly. So that means you are *out*."

Meaghan said, "But sometimes we get to have a second chance. Because I know how to spell the word."

Miss Bruce didn't smile. She didn't even blink. She shook her head and said, "I believe it's very important to be thinking all the time. That's what I expect of myself, and I expect it of every one of you, too. I'm sorry, but you are *out*."

Miss Bruce looked down at the seating chart, but I kept looking at Meaghan. I felt bad for her. She was chewing on her bottom lip. She looked like she might even cry.

Miss Bruce looked up from the chart. She looked right at Willie and said, "Philip, the word is 'mouse.'"

Willie smiled and said, "Um, Miss Bruce? Everyone calls me Willie, 'cause my last name is Willis. And I like Willie better than Philip too. So you can call me Willie."

Miss Bruce looked at Willie and said, "When we get to know each other a little better, then perhaps I'll use your nickname. But for now, I'd like to use your real name, all right? Now, Philip, the first word is '*mouse.*'"

For a second Willie looked like he thought Miss Bruce was kidding about calling him Philip. But she just stood there with her eyebrows up, waiting. Then he knew it was for real.

Willie was so surprised he didn't know what to do. So he gulped once or twice. And then he gulped some more.

Miss Bruce said, "I guess Philip is not ready to play, so for this round Philip is *out*." She looked down at the seating chart again, and then she looked right at me. "Jake, the first word is '*mouse*.'"

Maybe it was the look on Meaghan's face. Maybe it was the way Willie sat there gulping. Or maybe it was the way Miss Bruce kept saying "*out*." I don't know what it was, but something inside my head snapped.

I looked right at Miss Bruce and in a high, squeaky voice I said, "Mouse: m-i-c-k-e-y; mouse."

It took a second before everyone figured out what I had spelled. Then it sounded like every kid in the room took a deep breath. And held it.

Miss Bruce stared at me through her big glasses. "That was *not* the right word!"

So I kept using my best Mickey Mouse voice, and I said, "Heh, heh—well then, I guess I'm *out*."

I also guessed I was in trouble. But part of me didn't care.

21

Miss Bruce's face turned bright red. The paper in her hands started to shake. She looked like a cat when it's about to pounce.

Then Miss Bruce took three steps toward my chair. She frowned and said, "Jake, that was *not* funny!"

I took a quick look around the room. Everyone was grinning. And Willie was about to explode.

Miss Bruce was wrong. It *was* funny. Very funny.

Did Miss Bruce start yelling at me? Did she tell me to march down to the principal's office? Did she say, "I'll see *you* after school, Jake Drake!"

No.

Miss Bruce looked down at the seating chart. She kept looking at it for about five seconds— the longest five seconds of my life. And all that time I kept watching her face.

Then Miss Bruce looked up and said, "Annie, the word is still *'mouse.'* Spell it, please— *correctly.*"

And after Annie spelled it, Miss Bruce just went on with the spelling bee. *She acted like nothing had happened!*

But something had happened—actually, two things had happened:

The first thing was, I had done something silly in front of the whole class. Everybody had almost laughed out loud—they thought I was really funny! That had never happened before, and I kind of liked it. Plus, I hadn't gotten in trouble. Amazing!

The second thing that happened was more like a mystery. Because I wasn't really sure it had happened. It had happened—that is, *maybe* it had happened—when Miss Bruce was looking down at her seating chart, when I was watching her face. And here's the mystery: I thought I saw something.

Something I'd never seen before.

There on Miss Bruce's face. Just for a second. And it had looked sort of like . . . a *smile*.

CHAPTER FOUR

SECRET INFORMATION

By the time we had library period on Monday, I was sure I'd made a mistake about what I saw on Friday. Miss Bruce smiling? Even a tiny little smile? No way.

All Monday morning we worked so hard. Miss Bruce pushed and pushed at us, every second. Math sheets, map skills, reading books, spelling drills. Even morning recess wasn't fun because we knew there was more work waiting for us. More work and no smiles.

But right before lunch we went to the library.

Library period was great. A whole hour and tons of books. And no Miss Bruce. I mean, she was there, but she had to leave us alone for a while.

When we got there, I waved at Mrs. Brattle because she was helping in the library. She smiled and waved back.

Then I went to look for my Robin Hood book.

Robin Hood was my favorite book back when I was in second grade. I had never checked it out, because then I probably would have finished reading it in two days. I only read it during library period. That way, it lasted longer. Like a good jawbreaker.

I knew right where to look, and the book was there.

All the soft chairs were filled up. Plus it was sort of noisy at the front of the media center. So I took my book to the back of the big room, where it was quiet.

I sat on the carpet between some shelves. I leaned against the wall. Then I opened the book, and there I was: Me and Robin Hood and Little John, riding our horses through Sherwood Forest.

I was really into the story when I heard someone say, "I have to talk with you." And the voice wasn't in my book. It was in the library.

And I knew that voice. It was Miss Bruce.

And I thought, *Great. I'm at the best part of my book, and she has to talk with me.*

I started to stand up. Then another voice said, "All right, Hannah. We can talk right here."

And I knew that voice too. It was Mrs. Brattle. On the other side of the bookshelves. Three feet away.

I guess I could have made a noise. Or I could have stood up and started to look at the books on the shelf so they would see me.

But I didn't. I thought maybe I'd get in trouble for being way in the back of the library. Maybe they'd both yell at me.

So I froze. I just sat there.

I tried not to listen. I even put my hands over my ears. But I heard them anyway.

Mrs. Brattle said, "Sorry I didn't have time to talk with you on Friday afternoon. How's everything going?"

Miss Bruce said, "Well, something happened

right before lunch on Friday . . . and I'm not sure what to do about it."

"Oh?" said Mrs. Brattle. "What happened?"

And what did Miss Bruce talk about? She talked about me. She told Mrs. Brattle all about my big joke during the spelling bee.

And sitting there, I couldn't believe my ears. You know how you can tell a lot from hearing someone's voice? Well, even without seeing her, I could tell Miss Bruce was smiling. Smiling!

She even giggled a little and said, "I wish you could have seen Jake's face. He was *so* funny! He's such a cutie. I almost cracked up!"

Mrs. Brattle said, "Well, it's a good thing you didn't. Once you start laughing along with the kids, things can get out of hand very quickly."

"That's what my college teacher said too," said Miss Bruce. "She told us that the rule is, 'Don't smile until Christmas.'"

Mrs. Brattle chuckled and said, "Yes, I learned that too, and it's a good rule, especially when you're just starting out. Or when you're a substitute. Sometimes all it takes is one smile, and the kids will think they can get away with anything."

It was quiet for a few seconds. Then Miss Bruce said, "What do you think? Should I do something about Jake?"

"Jake?" said Mrs. Brattle. "Don't worry. He's a good boy. Still, you'll have to keep your eye on him. But if that's your biggest problem, then it sounds like you're doing just fine. Now, we'd better get back up front to the kids. It's getting a little too loud up there."

Then their voices got softer as they walked away.

I sat there on the floor. My heart was pounding. My mouth was dry.

I crawled forward and peeked around the corner of the shelf. When no one was looking, I slipped out and moved to a different part of the library.

I felt like a second-grade spy. And now I had some secret information: Miss Bruce wasn't an alien. She knew how to smile. And giggle.

Plus, she thought I was a cutie.

And best of all, she thought I was *funny*.

When you're only eight years old, and you get this kind of secret information, it can start something.

And that something is called trouble.

CHAPTER FIVE

UNSTOPPABLE

All during lunch on Monday, I wanted to tell Willie. I wanted to tell him that Miss Bruce was a giggler. And that I was a cutie.

But I didn't. Because the best part of a secret is the part that makes it a secret. And that's keeping it.

Back in our room after lunch recess, I wasn't sure what to do. So for a while I didn't do anything. Except more work. Because right after lunch we had silent reading.

Miss Bruce told us to read a story in our reading books. Anyone who finished was supposed to read a second story. And anyone who finished the second story was supposed to read a third story. That way, the fast readers would keep busy while the slow readers were finishing the first story.

And then when everyone was done reading the first story, we were going to talk about it.

I was a pretty fast reader back in second grade, so I was almost done with the third story when Miss Bruce clapped her hands twice and said, "All right, class. Everyone please turn to page 77 in your reading book. Let's begin by talking about *who* was in this story." Miss Bruce looked down at the seating chart and said, "Andrea, can you tell us the name of one person who was in the story?"

And Andrea did. She said, "Jim."

Which wasn't so hard. There were only three people in the whole story. And the story was only twelve pages long. Plus it had lots of pictures.

Then Carlos told the next *who,* and Lisa told the last *who.*

So we were done with the *who* part. Which

had been pretty boring. I thought Mrs. Brattle would have done it better.

But that's why Miss Bruce was there. So she could learn to be less boring. Someday. Maybe.

After the *who* came the *where*.

Miss Bruce said, "Now, tell the class *where* the story happened, Link."

Which was also super easy.

Except Link wasn't listening.

Link shoved something under the table and looked at Miss Bruce. And Link had that look in his eyes: the lost look.

Link said, "Um . . . where? Oh, yeah . . . where. Um . . . what was the question?"

Miss Bruce tilted her head and looked down at where Link had his hands under the table. Then her eyes got narrow and she pushed her lips together.

And I knew what was going to happen next. I could see it all: Miss Bruce was going to walk over and hold out her hand. Then she would say, "Link, give me that." And Link would pull out a comic book, or a toy, or something else really stupid. Then Miss Bruce would stare at him until he was really scared. She would make Link feel bad about not paying attention. Just like she had done to Laura and Meaghan.

Back in second grade, Link wasn't very nice. Most of the time he was a bully. So it wasn't very often that I felt sorry for Link.

But I did. At that moment, I felt sorry for him. And I felt sort of mad at Miss Bruce. Because I felt like she was sort of being a bully too.

So before Miss Bruce had a chance to walk over to Link, I raised my hand and started waving it around.

Miss Bruce turned and looked at me.

She didn't want to call on me. I could tell she wasn't done with Link. I kept waving my hand in the air anyway.

So Miss Bruce said, "Yes, Jake?" She knew my name without looking at the seating chart.

I said, "I think I know where the story happened."

Miss Bruce wasn't sure what to do. She wanted to go after Link, but now she had called on me, and I had an answer. So she said, "Well, then . . . then tell us, Jake. Where?"

"Well . . . ," I said slowly, "I'm not *exactly* sure . . ."

She said quickly, "Then just tell us where you *think* the story happened, Jake." Miss Bruce wanted to finish with me and get back to Link.

I said, "So I should just tell you? Like right now?"

She nodded her head at me.

Even slower, I said, "Even if I'm not *completely* sure?"

Miss Bruce said, "Yes, Jake. Even if it's only a guess. *Where* do you think this story happened?"

I looked Miss Bruce right in the eye and I said, "Well, I . . . I *think* it happened . . . on Earth!"

I kept staring into Miss Bruce's eyes. I heard a girl behind me giggle. But I didn't smile. I tried not to blink. I just waited.

Every kid in the room knew I had made a joke. Miss Bruce knew it too. But I kept acting like I was serious.

If she still thought I was a cutie, Miss Bruce did a good job of not showing it. She pushed her lips together into a thin line and glared at me. Then she said, "Yes. That's true. Of *course* the story happened on Earth, Jake." No smile. Not even a hint.

She turned back to Link. And now Link had his hand up. Whatever he had been hiding under the desk was gone.

Miss Bruce nodded at him and Link said, "The story happened by the ocean, right?"

"Yes, Link," said Miss Bruce. Then she took a deep breath. I thought she was going to walk over to Link and get mad at him anyway. Or maybe she would turn and get mad at me.

But she didn't. She let out her deep breath. Then she looked down at her seating chart again. She said, "Now, Ted, can you tell me *what* happened in our story?"

Ted was having a hard time. The corners of his mouth were wiggling. He wanted to smile, but he knew he'd better not.

I looked around the room. Half the kids in the class were smiling, and the other half were trying not to, like Ted.

There was only one person in the whole room who wasn't having any fun. And that was Miss Bruce.

But I wasn't thinking about Miss Bruce, not right then. I was too busy. I was enjoying myself. Because for the second time in two days, I'd done something funny. And I'd gotten away with it both times!

I was the new class clown. I was unstoppable.

CHAPTER SIX

MR. FUNNY BONE

When I got home from school on Monday after-noon, I asked my mom if I could have a snack. Because being so funny had made me hungry.

So Mom made me some peanut butter on crackers. Plus a glass of milk.

As I was eating I started to think. I tried to remember other times I had been funny at school. Like back when I was in first grade. Or kindergarten. I tried to remember. And I couldn't think of any.

And now, all of sudden, I had made everyone

want to start laughing—twice! And it had been so easy. I hadn't even been trying that hard.

I stopped right in the middle of drinking my milk. And I thought to myself, *If you're this funny without even trying, think how funny you could be if you worked at it!* I decided I could probably become the funniest kid in the history of the universe! And I could start the very next day!

If I was going to be super funny, I'd need super jokes. And I'd have to tell them just right.

So I went to find Abby. She's my little sister. When I was in second grade, Abby was in kindergarten. I found her in her room listening to a story cassette of *The Three Little Pigs*.

I went over to the cassette player and shut it off.

Abby said, "Hey! Put it back on!"

"Wait," I said, "because I want to try telling you some jokes. Okay?"

Abby crossed her arms and frowned. "I don't want jokes. I want the pigs."

"C'mon," I said. "It'll be fun. Are you ready?"

Abby scratched her knee. And made a face at the ceiling. And sat up on the edge of her bed. Then she said, "Okay."

So I said, "Knock, knock."

Abby wrinkled her nose. She said, "What?"

"I said, 'Knock, knock.' You know—it's a knock-knock joke."

Abby shook her head. "That's not funny."

"That's 'cause the joke's not over yet. Listen," I said. "I say 'Knock, knock,' then you say 'Who's there?', okay?" Then I said, "Knock, knock."

And Abby said, "Who's there, okay?"

"No," I said. "You just say 'Who's there?' That's all you say. Just 'Who's there?' Now, let's try it again. Ready?"

Abby nodded her head.

So I said, "Knock, knock."

And Abby said, "Who's there?"

And I said, "Toodle."

And Abby laughed. She clapped her hands and said, "Toodle's funny. Tell another one."

"No, no," I said. "'Toodle' isn't the funny part. I say 'Knock, knock.' Then you say 'Who's there?' Then I say 'Toodle,' and then you say 'Toodle *who?*' and *then* I finish the joke."

Abby looked at me. She said, "Toodle *was* funny. I don't want more joke."

"C'mon," I said. "I have to finish it, okay? I'm going to start over again."

Abby frowned. "Don't want to."

But I said, "Knock, knock."

And Abby said, "Who's there, okay?"

"No!" I yelled. "You just say 'Who's there?' Get it right, Abby!"

Abby shook her head. And then she yelled, "Mommeeee! MOMMEEEE!" Abby can really yell.

Mom ran up the stairs and into Abby's room in about two seconds. "What's the matter—are you hurt?" Then Mom saw me. She said, "Oh! Jake. Good. You're here too. Is everyone all right? Why did you call me like that, Abby?"

Abby pointed at me. "Because of him. He won't stop making a joke."

Mom frowned at me. "Have you been teasing Abby again, Jake?"

"No!" I said. "I'm not teasing her. I'm just trying to tell one stupid little knock-knock joke. And she can't even do it. And it's driving me crazy!"

Mom said, "Well, why don't you tell me the knock-knock joke. Then Abby can listen and see how it works, all right?"

41

I said, "Okay. Knock, knock."

And Mom said, "Who's there?"

And I said, "Toodle."

And Mom said, "Toodle who?"

And I said, "Toodle-oo to you too!"

Mom smiled and nodded. She said, "That's a good one."

Abby shook her head. "No. Just toodle. Toodle was better."

And that's when I went to my room. To practice telling jokes by myself.

I stood in front of the mirror that's above my dresser. I looked at myself and I started telling jokes.

Knock, knock.
Who's there?
Seven, eight, nine.
Seven, eight, nine who?
Sven ate nine cookies!

Knock, knock.
Who's there?
Robins go.

Robins go who?
No! Robins go tweet; *owls* go who!

What goes "Ha Ha bonk"?
A man who laughs his head off!

If I had five baseballs in one hand,
   and I had five baseballs in the other,
   what would I have?
Really BIG hands!

What's worse than finding a worm in
   your apple?
Finding half a worm!

It's not much fun telling jokes to yourself, so I got tired of that pretty fast. But as I looked in the mirror, I remembered how great I am at making funny faces.

So I practiced crossing my eyes and sticking my tongue out. I practiced pushing my nose up and making a pig face. I practiced puffing up my cheeks and pulling my eyelids out of shape. No doubt about it: I was a pretty funny kid.

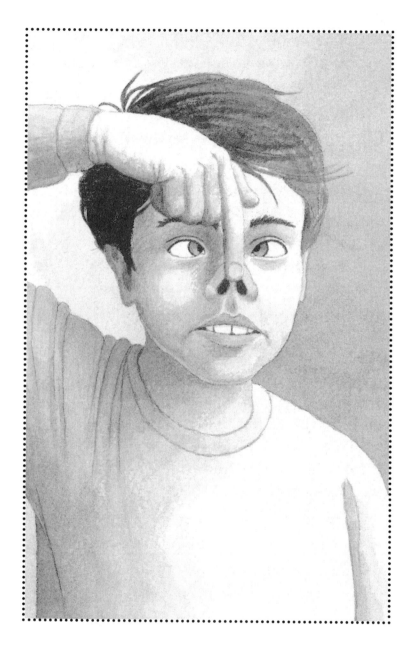

But after a while my face got tired. And my eyes started to hurt from crossing them so much.

So I looked on my bookshelf until I found this book of jokes I got at a book fair. And I sat on my bed and I read the whole book. Then I lay down on my stomach and read it again. The whole book.

I guess being so funny had made me tired, because I fell asleep with my face in the joke book. And the next thing I knew, Mom was calling to me to come downstairs for dinner.

When I went into the kitchen, my dad smiled at me and said, "Hey, Jake! What's new?"

And I said, "The moon."

Dad said, "The moon?"

And I said, "Yup. There's a new moon every month."

Dad and Mom laughed, and Dad said, "That's a good one, Jake."

Abby said, "It's not as funny as toodle."

We all sat at the table and I looked at the food. Right away I said, "Hey, Mom, know what they make from lazy cows? Meatloaf! Get it? Loaf? Like lazy? I just made that up! Pretty funny, huh?"

Mom smiled and nodded as she passed the potatoes. "Yes, pretty funny, Jake."

Then I said, "Hey, Dad, know how come the farmer ran a steamroller across his fields?"

Dad smiled and shook his head. So I said, "Because he wanted to grow some mashed potatoes!"

Dad laughed and said, "Mashed potatoes! That's a good one!"

All during dinner the jokes just kept on coming. It was like anything I looked at turned into a joke. Sometimes I remembered jokes, and sometimes I made up new ones. I even made my fish face at Abby when she was drinking her milk. Which made a big mess. But that was funny too!

When we had dessert, I said, "Hey, Dad, do you use your right hand or your left hand when you eat ice cream?"

"I guess I use my right hand."

And I said, "That's funny—I always use a *spoon!*"

I was hilarious!

When I asked to be excused, Dad said, "You sure are Mr. Funny Bone tonight, Jake. How'd all this get started?"

And like a dope I said, "Oh, it started at school."

Wrong thing to say.

Right away Dad frowned. He said, "Well, I hope you're getting it all out of your system before tomorrow morning. Being funny like this at school isn't a good idea, Jake. You understand that, right?"

And I nodded and I said, "Oh, I know that." And that was true. Because I knew it wasn't a good idea.

No, being funny at school on Tuesday wasn't a *good* idea: It was a *great* idea!

CHAPTER SEVEN

CHRISTMAS IN APRIL

On Tuesday morning Miss Bruce piled on the work. All my practice being Mr. Funny Bone wasn't any help at all. We had so much to do that I didn't have a chance to tell a single joke.

Plus, Miss Bruce was acting grumpier and grumpier.

When we were doing some math work, Carlos got up and started walking to the back of the room.

Miss Bruce looked at him and said, "Carlos, please stay in your seat and keep working. Math time is almost over."

He held up his pencil. "Gotta sharpen this."

Miss Bruce said, "I'm sure it's fine for now. Please keep working."

Carlos said, "But my pencil has to be extra sharp when I do math. It helps me make good numbers."

Miss Bruce said, "What did I tell you to do, Carlos?"

Carlos said, "You told me to sit down. But I need my pencil sharper. Honest."

Miss Bruce said, "You're wasting time, Carlos, and you have to finish all your math problems. So sit. Get back to work. Now."

Carlos walked slowly back to his chair and sat down.

Right away Annie reached across the table and handed Carlos a pencil.

Miss Bruce looked at Annie and she said, "Annie! *What* are you doing?"

Annie froze. She couldn't speak.

Miss Bruce said, "Annie, answer me!"

So Annie sort of hunched her shoulders and said, "I had an extra pencil. A sharp one."

Miss Bruce frowned, and I thought she was

going to start yelling. But she said, "Fine. That was very nice of you, Annie. Now, get back to work, both of you. Because anyone who does not finish all the math problems will have to stay in during recess."

Miss Bruce was acting so grumpy that I kind of got scared again. It was like my dad had said: Trying to be funny at school didn't seem like a good idea. I wanted to tell some jokes, but I didn't want to run in front of a train. And at that moment Miss Bruce seemed a lot like a locomotive.

So I finished my math problems, and so did everyone else. Then Miss Bruce told us to take out our spelling workbooks. And we did. And then Miss Bruce told us to turn to page 62. And we did. And we got right to work.

The spelling work was easy. It's the kind of work that leaves plenty of room inside your head for other stuff. So I started thinking about how funny I had been at dinner the night before.

And sitting there copying over words that end with "tch," I remembered something I'd forgotten to practice at home. Something very funny. Something I'm great at: noises.

Like my mouth-pops. I can make this really loud POP by pulling my tongue off the roof of my mouth. It's a great noise.

And I also make a good duck sound. I can quack by pushing air out of one side of my mouth. Plus I can laugh sort of like Donald Duck.

But my best sound is the one I always practice when Willie and I have sleepovers. And that's burping. Willie's a pretty good burper too, but I'm a better burper.

To make a big burp, all you have to do is gulp some air down into your stomach. And then you let it come back out as a burp. Simple.

So I was sitting there on that Tuesday morning doing my spelling work. Plus thinking about burping.

I wrote *patch*. And then I took a gulp of air.

I wrote *catch*. And I took a gulp of air.

I wrote *latch*. And I took a gulp of air.

I wrote *pitch*. Another gulp of air.

I wrote *ditch*. And I took one more gulp of air.

It wasn't until I took that fifth gulp of air that I remembered something. I wasn't at a sleepover at Willie's house. I was at school.

I straightened up in my chair and leaned back a little. It felt like I had a balloon stuffed under my T-shirt. But it wasn't a balloon. It was my stomach. I tapped on it with my pencil. It made a hollow sound, sort of like a tom-tom.

And that's when Miss Bruce came right up behind me and said, "Are you all done with your work, Jake?"

I turned around real fast and looked up into her face. And I said, "Nope."

That's what I *tried* to say. But I *actually* said, "NOOOOOOOOOOOOOOOOOOOOOOOOOOOPE."

It was the longest, loudest burp of my life!

The classroom was completely quiet. Everyone stared at me. Including Miss Bruce.

Don't ask me how I got the idea to do what I did next, because I don't know. There was Miss Bruce with her arms folded, looking down at me through her huge black glasses, and what did I do? I patted my chest, and I crossed my eyes, and I said, "Pardon me! It must have been that frog I ate for breakfast!"

Miss Bruce stood there. She was trying to get mad. She wanted to frown and yell and shake her finger at me and tell me that I had been terribly, terribly rude.

But she couldn't. I was just too funny. Plus I was a cutie.

So what did Miss Bruce do? She smiled! And it wasn't a little smile. It was a great big smile with teeth and everything. It was almost a grin. Every kid in the class saw that smile. And they also heard her giggle.

Miss Bruce's teacher at college had said, "Don't smile until Christmas." On that April morning, I was Santa Claus. Christmas had arrived!

After Miss Bruce smiled and giggled, everybody laughed a little. Then Miss Bruce covered her mouth with her hand and shook her head. And she tried to look serious again.

She said, "Let's not get silly, class. Please keep working on your spelling." And it almost worked. We all started to quiet down.

Then Willie burped almost as loud as I had and said, "I had *two* frogs for breakfast!"

All the kids laughed at that, much louder, and Susan Tuttle said, "Oooh! Gross!"

When a class starts laughing, it's sort of like when a volcano begins to rumble. Because it doesn't seem like much at first, but it's still dangerous.

Miss Bruce clapped her hands twice and said, "Class, that's enough!"

But the class didn't think it was enough. We were just getting started.

Link Baxter stood up and put his hands up under his arms and started hopping around the back of the room. "Hey, look! Look! I'm a frog. Ribbet! Ribbet!"

Miss Bruce clapped again. "Link, sit down! All of you, be quiet!"

No one was listening. Willie was still burping. Link was still hopping around the back of the room.

Then Ted tossed a ball of paper at Ben, and Ben threw it back to him. Carlos waved his arms and called, "Hey, Ted! Ted! Over here!"

And they started to play keep-away while Annie and Meaghan called out "Yay, Ben! Yay, Carlos! Hey, toss it to us, too!"

Miss Bruce shouted, "QUIET!"

But it kept getting louder and louder and louder. Our room had turned into an erupting volcano of laughing and shouting and goofing around.

And once that kind of volcano gets going, there's usually only one thing that can stop it: a real teacher.

Except there is one other way to plug the volcano. I saw it happen that morning.

Because if a student teacher stamps her feet and screams, "Stop it! Stop it!" and then bursts out crying and runs out of the classroom and slams the door, the volcano shuts down. And the room gets quiet.

Very, very quiet.

CHAPTER EIGHT

JUDGE BRATTLE

Mrs. Brattle walked into the room two minutes after Miss Bruce had run out.

Twenty-three kids were doing spelling work.

Silently.

No one even looked up at Mrs. Brattle. No one dared.

Mrs. Brattle sat down at the front of the room. She tapped a pencil on her desk and said, "Please stop working."

When we were all looking at her, she said,

"Now, who will tell me what happened in here? With Miss Bruce."

Mrs. Brattle was wearing a white shirt and a black sweater. She looked like a lady judge on one of those TV shows. Judge Brattle. She tapped her pencil on her desk again and looked around the room. She said, "I'm waiting. . . ."

I wanted to stand up and say, "Your Honor, it was all my fault. I'm just too funny. And I knew that Miss Bruce was a secret giggler. And I didn't mean to burp, but after I did, I said that thing about the frog. And that's what got everything so crazy. And I'm sorry that I'm so hilarious."

But I didn't say that. I didn't say anything.

Instead, Marsha McCall raised her hand. And when Mrs. Brattle called on her, Marsha started talking. And she talked in questions like she always does. She said, "Well, we were working on our spelling lessons? Because you know how it's Tuesday? And you know Miss Bruce? How she started laughing after Jake burped? Well, you know how it's hard to stop laughing sometimes? Don't you think maybe that's what happened? That everybody couldn't stop laughing?"

Marsha said a lot of words, but Mrs. Brattle only heard three of them. Mrs. Brattle turned and looked at me. And she said, "'After Jake burped?' Did Marsha just say 'after Jake burped'? Tell me a little more about that part of the story, Jake."

So I said, "I didn't mean to. But I did. Burp. And it was a big burp too. And then I said something funny."

Mrs. Brattle raised her eyebrows. She said, "Something funny?"

I nodded. "Yeah. I guess it was funny. I said it must have been the frog I ate for breakfast."

The corners of Mrs. Brattle's mouth wiggled a little, but she didn't smile. She said, "I see. And then what happened?"

"It just started to get silly. In the room. After Miss Bruce smiled. Because she never smiled at all until then. Not even once. And then she laughed a little too. And then . . . it got loud. That's all."

I guess I could have told Mrs. Brattle how Ted and Ben had been throwing stuff and how the girls had been yelling and how Willie had kept burping and Link kept hopping around.

But I didn't. Because I knew none of that would have happened if I hadn't been so funny. It was all my fault.

I guess that's what Mrs. Brattle thought too. Because she stood up and said, "Class, Mrs. Reed is on her way here. While she's here, I want you to finish your spelling and then you may do some silent reading. *Silent* reading."

Then she turned and looked at me. She said, "Jake, stand up. You're coming with me."

As we walked out of the courtroom, Judge Brattle didn't smile.

And neither did I.

CHAPTER NINE

NO MORE CLOWNING

I thought Judge Brattle was taking me to jail. Which would have been the principal's office.

So I was surprised when she marched right past the office. Instead, she stopped at a door marked TEACHERS' ROOM. She opened the door and said, "In here, Jake."

I'd never been in the teachers' room before. It was pretty nice in there. There was a big couch and a refrigerator. There was a little table in front of the couch with some magazines on it. One wall was covered with a huge bulletin board. Which was kind of messy. There was a big bookcase. There was even a Coke machine. Definitely the best room in the whole school.

And sitting at the big table in the middle of the room was Miss Bruce. With a box of tissues. And a red nose.

Miss Bruce's big glasses were next to the box of tissues. Without her glasses on, Miss Bruce looked like she was in high school. Just a girl with puffy eyes and a runny nose.

Mrs. Brattle pulled out a chair for me across from Miss Bruce. She walked around the table and sat down next to her student teacher.

Then Mrs. Brattle said, "Jake, is there something you want to say to Miss Bruce?"

I wanted to say, "Knock, knock." Because Miss Bruce looked like she needed a joke to cheer her up. But I knew that wasn't a good idea. So I said what Mrs. Brattle wanted me to. I said, "I'm sorry I was so funny in class. And I'm sorry I made you giggle. By being so funny."

Miss Bruce dabbed at her eyes and said, "It's okay, Jake. I'm sorry I got so upset. I didn't want

to. And I shouldn't have. But it's all over now. So it's okay."

Mrs. Brattle shook her head and said, "Actually, it's not okay, Miss Bruce. Jake shouldn't have been trying to do anything except be good and get his work done. Right, Jake?" I nodded. "And if you make a rude noise by mistake, then all you need to say is 'Excuse me.' Is that clear?" I nodded again. Mrs. Brattle narrowed her eyes and looked right into my face. "Jake, it *was* a mistake, right? When you burped?"

And I looked right back into Mrs. Brattle's eyes. And I was so glad that I could tell the truth, because Judge Brattle would have been able to tell I was lying. I said, "Yes. I didn't burp on purpose."

Mrs. Brattle nodded. "I'm glad to know that, at least. But the silliness has got to stop. Now. Do you understand?"

I nodded. "Uh-huh. No more silliness."

Mrs. Brattle said, "All right, then. Miss Bruce, is there anything else you want to say?"

Miss Bruce shook her head. She looked a lot better. But I could still tell she had been crying. She said, "No. Nothing else."

Then Mrs. Brattle said, "Jake, how about you? Anything else?"

It was one of those times when I should have known to keep my mouth shut. I should have just shaken my head and sat there looking scared. Or maybe I should have whispered "No, thank you," and folded my hands in my lap. But I didn't.

I looked right at Miss Bruce and I said, "Miss Bruce, how come you never smiled until today? Was that because of what your teacher said? About Christmas?"

Oops. BIG oops! The second I said that I knew I had made a major goof.

Miss Bruce's eyes opened wide. And so did Mrs. Brattle's. They both looked at me. And then they looked at each other. And then back at me. Mrs. Brattle folded her arms.

And I knew they knew. They knew I had heard them talking that day in the library.

Miss Bruce sat up straight in her chair. Even without the big glasses, her eyes were plenty scary. She said, "Why . . . why you little *sneak!* You were *spying* on me!" I was glad she was over on the other side of the big table.

I gulped and said real fast, "No, really, I wasn't spying! That day in the library? I didn't mean to hear you talking. I didn't do it on purpose. I was just sitting there reading *Robin Hood*, and you came to where I was, and I was afraid I'd get in trouble for sitting in the back, and then you started talking. You just started talking! I tried not to listen. But I heard you anyway. I didn't mean to. And I didn't tell anyone about it. Honest! And I'm sorry." I was looking back and forth between their faces.

I could tell they believed me. But I still felt like Miss Bruce was going to jump over the table and come after me.

Mrs. Brattle took charge. She said, "Seems like you have quite a lot to be sorry about today, Jake. But I think Miss Bruce and I understand the situation. And, if Miss Bruce will accept your apology, then so will I, and we'll just put all of this business behind us. All right, Miss Bruce?"

Miss Bruce nodded. But it wasn't a very big nod.

"Very well, then," said Mrs. Brattle, standing up. "Then let's get you two back to class."

Miss Bruce kind of jumped a little in her chair.

"Me?" she asked. "You mean I have to go back? To your class? Today?"

Mrs. Brattle looked down at Miss Bruce and smiled. "Why, of course you do. Right now. You're the teacher."

Miss Bruce looked like someone had just told her to go for a walk in a graveyard. At midnight. Without a flashlight. She was scared.

And then I got it: She was scared of *us*—of the kids! Of noise and silliness and craziness! Miss Bruce was scared, and Mrs. Brattle wasn't. Because Mrs. Brattle was a real teacher.

Miss Bruce bit her lip. She looked at Mrs. Brattle and said, "Don't you think you should come with me?"

Mrs. Brattle shook her head. "No, you'll be fine. The class will be waiting to see what happened to Jake, and Jake is going to look like he's had a good scolding. Jake is also going to be a perfect *angel* from this moment on. And *you* are going to walk back into that room and show all the boys and girls that just because you smile once in a while does not mean that they can go wild and misbehave."

Miss Bruce said, "But . . . but I *cried*. All those kids saw me cry and run out of the room! I *can't* go back."

Mrs. Brattle smiled and patted Miss Bruce on the arm. "Don't worry, dear. Everyone understands about crying, especially children. When it happens, you dry your face off, and then you go on with whatever you have to do. And *you* have a class to teach."

Then Mrs. Brattle took hold of the back of Miss Bruce's chair, so Miss Bruce had to stand up.

"There we go," said Mrs. Brattle. "Now, you and Jake run along. Mrs. Reed is needed back in the library. And Jake, from now on, I want nothing but good news about you, is that clear?"

I nodded.

And then Miss Bruce and I walked down the hall to our classroom.

I did what Mrs. Brattle said. I walked into the room. I sat down. I didn't look at anybody. I didn't smile. I tried to look like I had just lived through the worst ten minutes of my life. I tried to look like I was happy just to be alive.

And it turned out that Mrs. Brattle was right. Not one kid tried to be silly. Not one kid was noisy or rude.

And Miss Bruce did great. After all that yelling and the crying and the running out of the room, she acted like it wasn't a big deal. And because she acted that way, it wasn't. It was like none of it had ever happened.

But it had happened. And I had the proof. Because I kept on being funny.

Except I was never funny in class. And not when Miss Bruce was around. Or Mrs. Brattle.

So mostly I was funny for Willie. Before school, at recess, in gym class, on Saturdays—every chance I got, I told Willie jokes and made funny noises and faces at him. At lunch one day I made a pig face, and Willie laughed so hard he snorted a chunk of Oreo right out of his nose! I was a riot!

But after about three weeks, Willie was starting to go crazy, and I was starting to run out of jokes. So one day I just stopped. And I'm glad I did, because it's hard to try to be funny *all* the time. It's much better to save up silliness for special occasions. Like sleepovers. Or long bus rides.

The rest of Miss Bruce's student-teaching time went by pretty fast. And the best part is she wasn't as grumpy or as picky or as fussy as before. It was like Miss Bruce didn't have to be that way anymore. Because she wasn't afraid. I guess if you can laugh and giggle, and then watch your class go nuts, and then scream and yell, and then run out of the room crying, and *then* come back and have everything be okay, there's not much left to be scared about.

Mrs. Brattle planned a surprise party for Miss Bruce at the end of her three weeks. We all signed a big card we made for her in art class. And when Mrs. Brattle gave her a book and a hug, I thought Miss Bruce was going to start crying and run out of the room again.

But she didn't. She blinked a lot. And then she smiled. It was a big smile, with teeth and everything. Her voice sounded wobbly. And she said, "I learned so much here at Despres Elementary School. And I know that no matter how many other places I go and no matter how many other children I teach, I'm never going to forget you."

Miss Bruce was talking to the whole class. But at the end, she looked right at me. And I got this feeling that what she meant was, she was never going to forget me: Jake Drake, Class Clown.